**A Timeless Story of
God's Love and Forgiveness**

THE **PRIEST** WITH **DIRTY** CLOTHES

# R.C. SPROUL

ILLUSTRATIONS BY **LIZ BONHAM**

Tommy
NELSON™

Thomas Nelson, Inc.
Nashville

*The Priest with Dirty Clothes*

Copyright © 1997 by R. C. Sproul for text.
Copyright © 1997 by Liz Bonham for illustrations.

Published in Nashville, Tennessee, by Tommy Nelson™, a division
of Thomas Nelson, Inc.

Managing Editor: Laura Minchew
Project Editor: Beverly Phillips

Scripture marked ICB is quoted from the *International Children's
Bible, New Century Version*, copyright © 1986, 1988 by Word
Publishing.

**Library of Congress Cataloging-in-Publication Data**
Sproul, R. C. (Robert Charles), 1939–
    The priest with dirty clothes / R. C. Sproul ; illustrated
by Liz Bonham.
        p.    cm.
    Summary: Grandfather tells Darby and Campbell the parable
of the priest who is not allowed to preach until he changes
the dirty clothes he is wearing for clean ones.
    ISBN 0-8499-1455-8
    [1. Christian life   Fiction. 2. Cleanliness   Fiction.
3. Parables.]  I. Bonham, Liz, ill.  II. Title.
PZ7.S7693Mi  1997                                97-14038
[E]   DC21                                       CIP
                                                 AC

*Printed in the United States of America*

97 98 99 00 01 02 RRD 9 8 7 6 5 4 3 2 1

# LETTER TO PARENTS

*The Priest with Dirty Clothes* is my attempt to help children understand one of the most difficult concepts of Christianity—how we are made acceptable to God through Christ's righteousness. By viewing their righteousness through Christ, it is my hope that children can begin to understand the glory of the Gospel.

This story is based on a favorite scripture, Zechariah, Chapter 3:1–5 . In this passage, Joshua, as High Priest of Israel, is standing before the Angel of the Lord wearing dirty clothes. The Angel of the Lord speaks to Joshua, telling him that he has been cleansed of his sin, and then replaces Joshua's dirty clothes with beautiful, clean garments. This scripture offers a beautiful illustration of how Christ cloaks us in His "garment" of righteousness so that we may stand faultless, or clean, before the throne of God.

Before reading this story to your children, please read the passage in Zechariah, and bear these thoughts in mind as you read. I pray that God will bless your efforts to show your children the love, grace, and forgiveness of God.

DR. R. C. SPROUL

# THE VISION OF THE HIGH PRIEST

Then he showed me Joshua the high priest. He was standing in front of the Lord's angel. And Satan was standing by Joshua's right side to accuse him. The Lord said to Satan, "The Lord says you are guilty, Satan. The Lord who has chosen Jerusalem says you are guilty. This man was like a burning stick pulled from the fire."

Joshua was standing in front of the angel. And Joshua was wearing dirty clothes. Then the angel spoke to those standing near him. He said, "Take those dirty clothes off Joshua."

Then the angel said to Joshua, "Look, I have taken away your sin. And I am giving you new clothes." Then I said, "Put a clean turban on his head." So they put a clean turban on his head. They also dressed him while the Lord's angel stood there.

ZECHARIAH 3:1–5 (ICB)

Darby and Campbell MacFarland lived near a beautiful lake in Scotland called Loch Lomond. It seemed seven-year-old Darby was always finding ways to get herself and her little brother, Campbell, in trouble. One day after it had rained, they went outside to play. "Let's make mud pies," Darby said.

The children pretended that they were bakers. They took some mud and rolled it, patted it, and fashioned it into pretend cakes and pies. As they played, they wiped their hands on their clothes spreading mud all over themselves. They laughed and giggled as they got themselves muddier and muddier.

When their mother saw them, she was not happy.
"Just look at you! You look like mud pies yourselves,"
she cried out. "Hurry and take off
those filthy clothes, and I'll give
you both a bath."

After the children were all clean, their mom looked at the muddy clothes. "I'll never be able to get these dirty clothes clean," she said to herself.

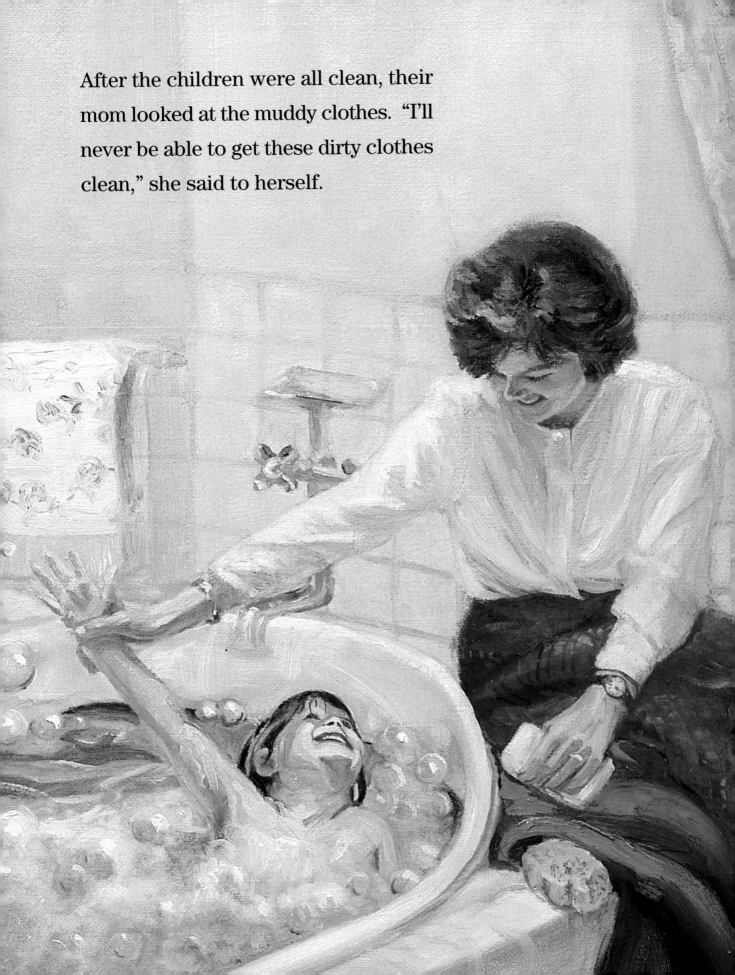

Just then there was a knock at the front door. It was the children's grandfather. As Darby and Campbell rushed in to hug him, Grandpa grinned and said, "It looks like someone made a mud pie bakery in the front yard." The kids giggled.

"It seems that our little bakers have ruined their clothes," said Mom.

"That's too bad," Grandpa said. "But it certainly reminds me of a strange and wonderful story."

"Oh, tell us, please," Darby begged, pulling Grandpa toward the sofa.

As soon as they were all seated, Grandpa began the story. . . .

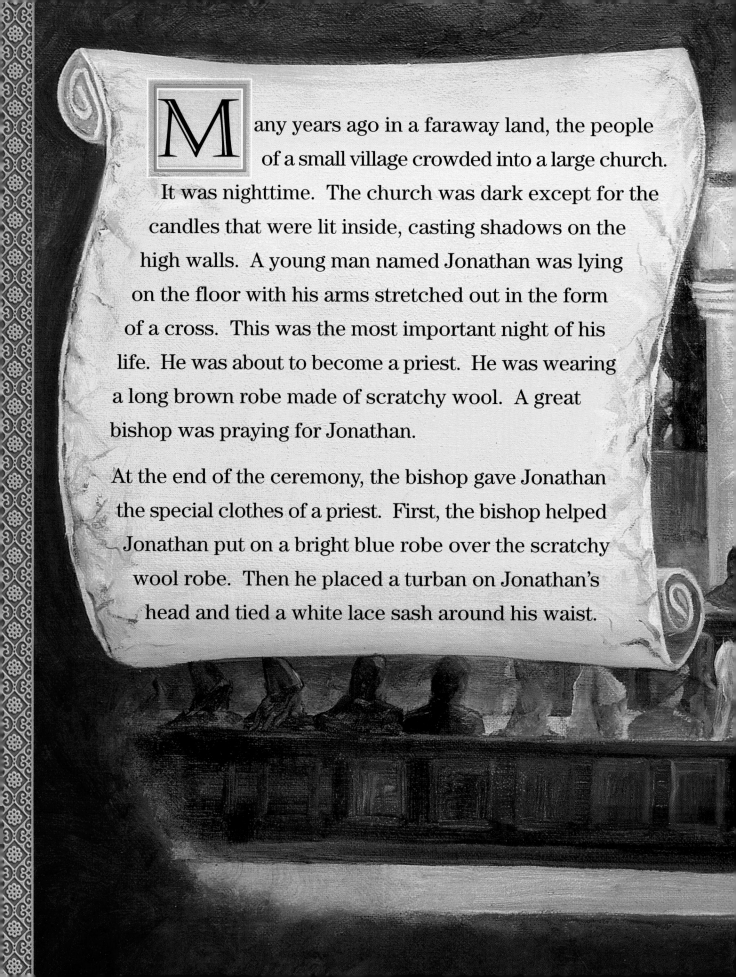

Many years ago in a faraway land, the people of a small village crowded into a large church. It was nighttime. The church was dark except for the candles that were lit inside, casting shadows on the high walls. A young man named Jonathan was lying on the floor with his arms stretched out in the form of a cross. This was the most important night of his life. He was about to become a priest. He was wearing a long brown robe made of scratchy wool. A great bishop was praying for Jonathan.

At the end of the ceremony, the bishop gave Jonathan the special clothes of a priest. First, the bishop helped Jonathan put on a bright blue robe over the scratchy wool robe. Then he placed a turban on Jonathan's head and tied a white lace sash around his waist.

The very next week, Jonathan was invited to the castle of the king. He would preach his first sermon to the royal household. Jonathan worked hard to prepare his sermon. He wanted it to be his very best.

When it was time for Jonathan to go to the castle, it was raining very hard. Jonathan was sad that his new special clothes would get wet as he rode his horse to the castle.

Jonathan tried to keep his new clothes from getting rained on by wearing a cape with a hood.

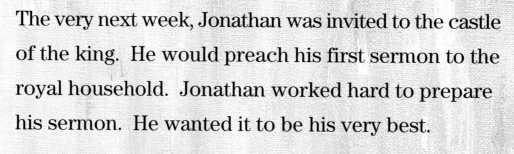

As Jonathan and his horse made their way to the castle, the muddy road became more and more slippery.  Suddenly, the horse stumbled and Jonathan fell off.

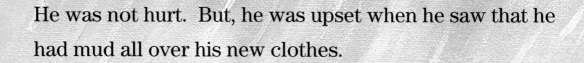

He was not hurt.  But, he was upset when he saw that he had mud all over his new clothes.

Jonathan had mud on his face and on his shoes.  He had mud all over his blue robe.  The white lace sash was no longer white, and his turban looked like a big mud cake.

Jonathan tried hard to clean himself off.  But there was no way he could clean his clothes and get to the castle on time. He thought about running away.  He didn't want to preach in front of the king looking like this.  *The king just has to understand*, he thought.  So Jonathan kept going until he reached the castle.

When he arrived, Jonathan hurried into the castle looking for a place to clean himself up. But he could not clean his dirty clothes. The tower bells began to ring. It was time for the royal household to gather to hear Jonathan's sermon. Slowly, Jonathan walked to the place where he was to stand and opened his Bible. As soon as the people saw him, they began whispering.

The king was surprised to see the priest wearing such dirty clothes. But the king was a kind and gentle ruler, and he could see that Jonathan was ashamed of the way his clothes looked. Knowing there must be a good reason for Jonathan's dirty clothes, the king motioned for Jonathan to begin.

As soon as Jonathan started to speak, the court magician, whose name was Malus, stood up and shouted, "Wait! You can't preach before the king wearing those dirty clothes."

Malus was a very mean man. He
hated all priests. He even hated priests
whose clothes were clean. Malus had
great power with the people. They
were afraid of him. As soon as Malus
shouted out against Jonathan, other
people began to yell mean things
about Jonathan too.

The king knew that this was not a good thing. The king felt sorry for Jonathan. He didn't like the way Malus was behaving. He was afraid that Malus might cause someone to harm the priest.

The king stood and said to the people, "Be calm. Please, stop talking. I will take care of this problem."

That very minute the people grew silent. Even Malus stopped talking. The king then looked at Jonathan and asked him to come forward. When Jonathan walked up to him, the king said, "Why did you come here looking so dirty?"

Jonathan explained what had happened. The king nodded and said, "I understand. I am sorry that you had this accident. But you cannot preach here today wearing such dirty clothes. You may come back next week and preach. I will give you another chance. But only if you come back wearing clean clothes."

"Thank you, Your Majesty," said Jonathan. "I am sorry I look so dirty. I promise that next week I will be clean."

With that, the king told Jonathan to go.
Jonathan left the castle as fast as he could.
When he got back home, the first thing he did
was try to clean his clothes. But the stains
were so deep he couldn't get them out.

The next day Jonathan took his special clothes to the town fuller. The fuller was a person who cleaned people's dirty clothes. He had special kinds of soaps that could get the mud out of clothing. The fuller looked at Jonathan's clothes and said, "These clothes are so dirty, I don't know if I can make them clean. But I will do my best. Come back tomorrow, and I will have them ready for you."

When Jonathan
returned to the fuller's shop,
the fuller said, "I am afraid that I
cannot make your clothes clean.  They are
ruined forever.  The only thing you can do now
is to get new clothes."

"But I can't get new clothes," Jonathan said.  "These
clothes were given to me by the bishop.  He only gives
out one set of clothes."

"I am sorry about that," said the fuller,  "but there is
nothing more I can do.  You should go to see the bishop.
 Maybe he can give you a new set of clothes so you can
preach before the king."

When Jonathan left the fuller's shop, he didn't think the bishop would give him a new set of clothes. But, he had to ask anyway. So he went straight to the bishop's office.

The bishop patiently listened to Jonathan's story of the accident. Then he said, "This is a sad thing that has happened to you, Jonathan. But there is nothing I can do to help you."

Jonathan was very sad. "Isn't there something I can do to get clean clothes? Please, let me do something special to earn new clothes."

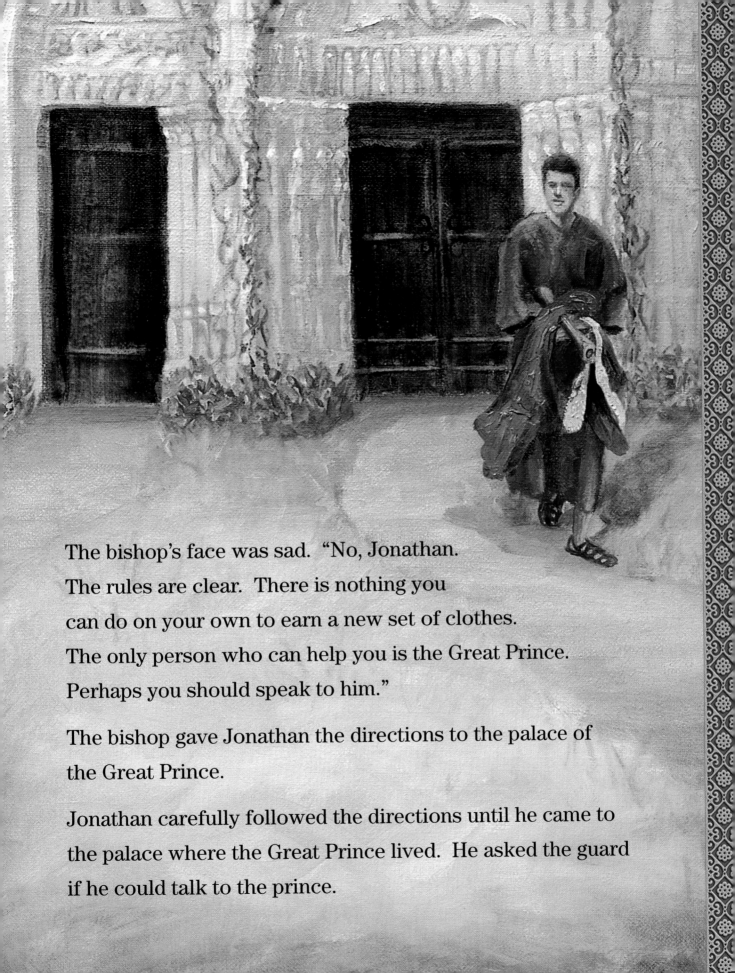

The bishop's face was sad. "No, Jonathan. The rules are clear. There is nothing you can do on your own to earn a new set of clothes. The only person who can help you is the Great Prince. Perhaps you should speak to him."

The bishop gave Jonathan the directions to the palace of the Great Prince.

Jonathan carefully followed the directions until he came to the palace where the Great Prince lived. He asked the guard if he could talk to the prince.

The guard walked Jonathan into the royal room where the prince was sitting on a throne.

When Jonathan saw the prince, he was amazed. He had never seen anyone who looked like this. He was dressed in a long purple robe with precious jewels on it. There was a band around his waist made of pure gold. He wore a turban that was as white as snow. His face seemed to shine like the sun.

The prince looked at Jonathan with caring eyes and asked, "Why are you here? What do you need from me?" His voice was soft and kind.

Jonathan asked carefully, "O Great Prince, I am a priest. I have ruined my clothes, and I cannot stand in front of the king without clean clothes. No one has been able to make my clothes clean. I have been sent to you to see if there is anything you can do to help me."

Jonathan told the prince the story of how he had gotten dirty. The prince listened quietly, and then said to Jonathan, "I understand your problem, and I can help you."

"Are you going to give me clean clothes?" asked Jonathan.

"You will soon see, Jonathan," the prince replied. "But first come with me to the fireplace."

Jonathan followed the prince to the corner of the room where a small fire was burning in the fireplace. Then the prince did a strange thing. He pointed to a small branch that was at the edge of the fire. The branch was not burning. It was charred but no longer hot. The prince told Jonathan to pick up the branch.

Jonathan reached out his hand to pick up the branch. It was cold and did no harm to him. When Jonathan put it down, the prince said, "Now look at your hand."

Jonathan looked down and saw that his hand was black. It was covered with soot from the branch.

"Jonathan," the prince said, "you are like the branch you pulled from the fire. You are covered with black dirt. But the dirt is not just on your clothes. It is on your heart. Sin, the wrongs that you do, makes your heart dirty. No soap can make it clean."

Then the prince said, "Jonathan, I can help you. Go to the castle next week and be ready to preach your sermon. Wear your dirty clothes, and I will take care of them."

Jonathan's heart felt sad, and he grew afraid. "But Great Prince, I was told by the king that I could not stand in front of him in my dirty clothes. And the evil magician, Malus, will do something mean to me if I enter the castle with dirty clothes."

A warm smile spread across the face of the Great Prince. "Yes, Jonathan, I know all about Malus and his meanness. I also know the king very well. You see, Jonathan, the king is my father."

Jonathan asked, "How are you going to make my clothes clean?"

The prince answered, "I promised you that I will take care of that. I never break my promises. I always do what I say I will do. Now you go home and get ready for your sermon. I will be there, and I will do what I promised."

When the next week came, Jonathan was both excited and a little afraid. Jonathan thought about not going to the castle at all. Then he remembered the promise the prince had made to him. "I will trust in the promise of the prince. I will go to the castle," he said to himself.

Jonathan went outside and got on his horse. This time the day was bright with sunshine. There were no storm clouds in the sky. Jonathan had no trouble making the journey to the castle.

When he got there, he could see a crowd of people going in. Jonathan swallowed hard and walked inside to the place where the priest stands. Again, before he could speak Malus stood up and shouted, "May bad things happen to you, O priest! You are still wearing dirty clothes!"

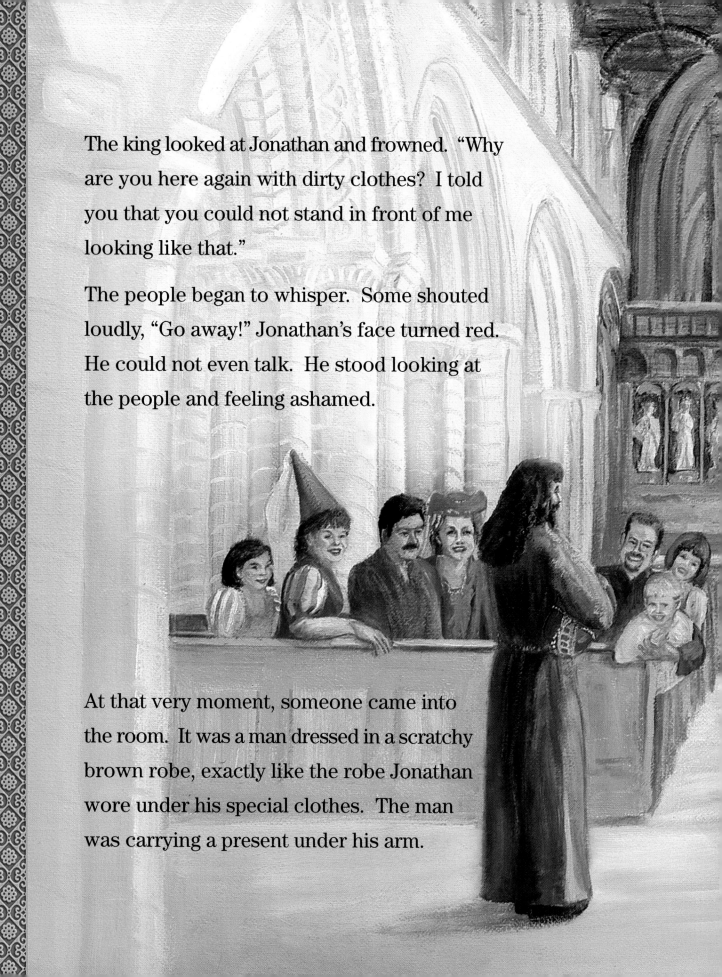

The king looked at Jonathan and frowned. "Why are you here again with dirty clothes? I told you that you could not stand in front of me looking like that."

The people began to whisper. Some shouted loudly, "Go away!" Jonathan's face turned red. He could not even talk. He stood looking at the people and feeling ashamed.

At that very moment, someone came into the room. It was a man dressed in a scratchy brown robe, exactly like the robe Jonathan wore under his special clothes. The man was carrying a present under his arm.

No one knew who the stranger was.
Then someone shouted, "It's the
Great Prince!"

Malus didn't know what to think.
He said, "What is the meaning of this?
Why are you here, and why are
you wearing that itchy robe?"

At first the prince did not answer. He was
smiling as he walked to the front of the
room and stood next to Jonathan. Then
he spoke to Jonathan saying, "Take off
your dirty clothes and give them to me."

Jonathan took off his dirty clothes, the special ones that the bishop had given him. Now, he stood before the king wearing only his own scratchy brown robe.

The prince took Jonathan's dirty clothes and put them on himself. Then he handed Jonathan the present and told him to open it. Everyone watched Jonathan as he carefully opened the present the prince had given him.

Jonathan's eyes grew wide when he saw what the present was. It was the perfect present. Inside were the beautiful clothes that belonged to the prince. The prince smiled again at Jonathan and said, "These are the clean clothes I promised you. There is not a spot of dirt on them. Put them on and preach your sermon."

Jonathan's hands shook as he put on the prince's beautiful clothes. The prince said to the king, "Father, may Jonathan now stand in your presence? He is one of my people."

The king was pleased and said to the prince, "Yes, my son. As long as he wears your clothes, he may stand in front of me."

Then the prince said to Jonathan, "These clothes are yours forever. They will never wear out and nothing can ever make them dirty. They are perfect for you."

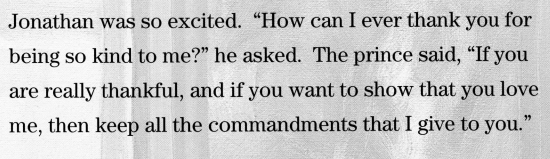

Jonathan was so excited. "How can I ever thank you for being so kind to me?" he asked. The prince said, "If you are really thankful, and if you want to show that you love me, then keep all the commandments that I give to you."

"Oh, I will," said Jonathan. "I want to be good enough to wear your clothes."

"But you cannot be good enough, Jonathan. You must live your whole life trusting in my goodness while you wear my clothes."

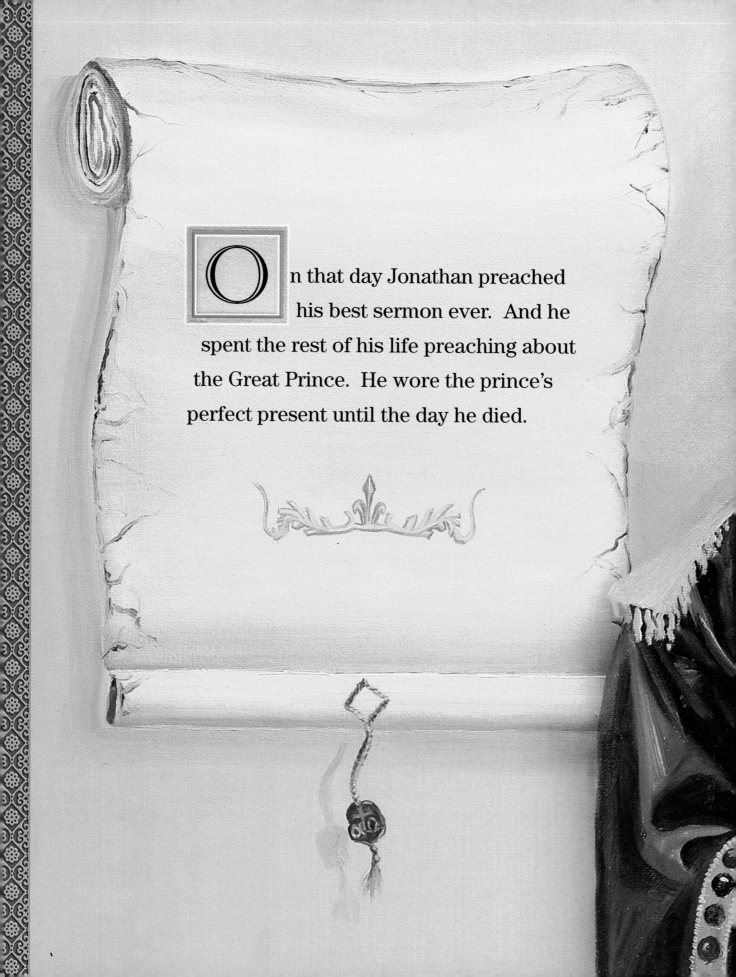

On that day Jonathan preached his best sermon ever. And he spent the rest of his life preaching about the Great Prince. He wore the prince's perfect present until the day he died.

Grandpa turned to Darby and Campbell and said, "That is the end of my story.  Did you like it?"

"Oh, yes," the children replied.  "Do you think that if we could find the Great Prince that He would give us clean clothes, too?"

"Yes," Grandpa answered.  "He gives clean clothes to everyone who believes in Him. But they are not clothes like the ones you ruined today.  The Great Prince gives new clothes for our hearts.

"The dirt that we get on our clothes can sometimes be washed clean. But we have a bigger problem.  When we sin and do wrong our hearts become so dirty that we cannot stand in front of God.  For us to be able to be friends with God, we need to have the dirt on our hearts cleaned.  This is what Jesus does for us.  He forgives us and takes the dirt from our hearts and puts it on Himself, just like the Great Prince took Jonathan's dirty clothes and wore them.

"So, when God looks at us, He doesn't see the dirt on our hearts. Instead, He sees a heart covered by His Son's clean clothes. If you trust in Jesus and believe His Word, your heart will be clean. Jesus will forgive you when you sin. But you have to ask Him to forgive you. Then, He cleans your heart, and you can stand in front of God forever."

"I'm sorry we got mud on our clothes. But I'm sure glad we heard the story about the Great Prince," said Darby.

With a hug, her mom said, "Yes, it is a story we all need to hear and remember."